For Aunt Ruth—ES
For Noah Drew, Selina Shefrin, Maddy Bossin and Davy Bossin with love—SES

Thanks to Nan and Smudge for the inspiration.—ES

Published simultaneously in 2006 in Great Britain and Canada
by **Tradewind Books Limited www.tradewindbooks.com**
Distribution and representation in Canada by Publishers Group Canada
Distribution and representation in the UK by Turnaround

Text copyright © 2006 by Ellen Schwartz
Illustrations copyright © 2006 by Sima Elizabeth Shefrin

Book design by Elisa Gutiérrez

This book was set in Cantoria for the text and Galahad for the title.

Origami instructions © 1998 by George Levenson

10   9   8   7   6   5   4   3   2   1
. . . .
LIBRARY AND ARCHIVES CANADA CATALOGUING IN PUBLICATION

Schwartz, Ellen, 1949-
    Abby's birds / by Ellen Schwartz ; illustrated by Sima Elizabeth Shefrin.

ISBN 1-896580-86-6

    1. Picture books for children. I. Shefrin, Sima Elizabeth, 1949-
II. Title.

PS8587.C578A63 2006   jC813'.54   C2006-902752-8
. . . .

Imaging and colour separation by Disc • Printed and bound in China

The publisher wishes to thank the Government of Canada and Canadian Heritage
for their financial support through the Canada Council for the Arts, the Book
Publishing Industry Development Program (BPIDP) and the Association for the
Export of Canadian Books. The publisher also wishes to thank the Government of
British Columbia for the financial support it has extended through the book publishing
tax credit program and the British Columbia Arts Council.

Abby's Birds

By **Ellen Schwartz**   *Illustrated by* **Sima Elizabeth Shefrin**

VANCOUVER

LONDON

NEW HOUSE. New backyard.

Abby dashed outside. She sniffed a violet, tapped
every fence post, threw her ball up high... higher...
chased it under a tall, leafy tree—

"Oh!" she said. "Who are you?"

An old woman was sitting in a wooden chair in the next-door yard. Round face, wrinkled face.

"I am Mrs. Naka."

"I'm Abby."

"How do you do, Abby?"

"Are you my new neighbour?"

"No, you are *my* new neighbour. I have lived here a lifetime."

"Are you old?"

"Very old."

Mrs. Naka smiled. Her face crinkled like tree bark.

A bird landed in the grass near them. Brownish-grey with a brick-red chest. It stabbed the grass, speared a wriggling worm, rose and vanished into the leaves.

Abby heard rustling. A quiet chirp.

Mrs. Naka smiled. "Robins have been building nests in this maple tree for as long as I can remember. Come, I will show you."

Leaning on a cane, Mrs. Naka limped slowly.

Abby made her steps go slow, too.

"Why do you have a cane?"

"My bones are fragile, like the birds'."

Abby thought of Mrs. Naka's bones snapping like slender birds' bones. She took Mrs. Naka's hand. Holding tight, Mrs. Naka pointed with her cane.

Abby looked up. All she saw was leaves and shadows.

"There it is!" Straws and twigs, woven into a brown bowl. "Are there babies?"

"Soon. Very soon."

Mrs. Naka's hair was loose, the brush moving in long downward strokes. She removed a tangle of white hair from the brush, let it go. Just before it floated to the ground, a robin plucked it out of the air.

"I want to give a hair, too!" Abby said. She tugged off her elastic. Curls sprang free. "Ouch!" She flung the hair upward.

The robin swooped and snatched it.

"My hair will be in the nest. With yours."

"A pillow for the baby birds," Mrs. Naka said.

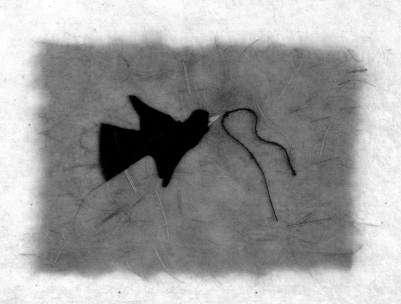

Abby coloured, her paper resting on the arm of Mrs. Naka's chair. The baby robins squawked hungrily from the treetop. Back and forth flew the mama and the papa, carrying insects.

Mrs. Naka held a piece of paper, fingers remembering. Then she began to fold.

Abby looked up. "Oh! Mrs. Naka, what is it?"

Mrs. Naka moved the folded paper down and up. Wings rose and fell, rose and fell.

"It's a bird!"

"Yes. *Tori*."

Abby's small fingers tried to copy what Mrs. Naka's nimble ones did. Her folds were crooked. The paper crinkled. Clicking her tongue, she smoothed out the paper, folded again. Finally she had a small, tattered bird.

Abby took the two birds, one in each hand. She moved her arms up and down. The birds soared on breaths of air. "They're flying, Mrs. Naka!"

"Yes."

Abby ran, her arms tracing great billowing curves. "Watch the *tori* fly!"

A baby robin lay beneath the tree, one wing bent like a broken fan.

"What happened?" Abby's voice trembled.

"It wasn't strong enough to fly," Mrs. Naka said.

"Is it…dead?"

"Yes."

Abby burst into tears, pushing her face into Mrs. Naka's waist.

Later, Abby dug a shallow grave. She placed a violet on top of the fresh dirt.

"Are the other babies safe?"

"Yes. They are strong. And next year they will come back to raise their own babies."

"New babies every year?"

"Year after year. Always."

That night, Abby dreamed she was a baby bird, perched on the rim of the nest. The ground was far. The sky was vast. She lifted her wings.

Flying, Abby didn't see Mrs. Naka climb onto a chair. She didn't hear the crash as the chair toppled. She didn't see the papers spread like a rainbow from Mrs. Naka's outflung arms.

Sirens, loud… louder—

Abby ran outside. Attendants were carrying Mrs. Naka to an ambulance.

"Mrs. Naka, what's the matter?"

"I fell. My hip is broken."

"Will you come home soon?"

Mrs. Naka sighed. "Not soon. First my bones must mend."

Tears trembled on Abby's lashes.

Mrs. Naka wiped Abby's cheek. "But I *will* come, Abby. Home to you and our tree."

"And the birds."

"Yes." Mrs. Naka held out a sheaf of paper. "For you. For *tori*."

As summer faded, Abby practised. She folded, unfolded.

The baby birds' chests turned from speckled to brown to orange. The chicks grew as big as their parents.

The maple leaves fell. One day, a robin flew away. Then another. Black-and-orange smudges overhead, flying toward the sun.

Abby made birds. Turquoise, violet, red.

Soon the branches were bare. The robins were gone.

On the day that Mrs. Naka was coming home, Abby carried folded papers and loops of string outside. Her mama and papa held the ladder for her.

When she was finished, Abby waited by the gate. She looked up the street, down the street.

"Mrs. Naka, you're home!"

Mrs. Naka's eyes disappeared into her smile.

"The birds flew away," Abby told her.

Mrs. Naka sighed. "No more birds until spring."

"Come see!"

Abby pushed Mrs. Naka to the maple tree. There, dangling from bare branches, were birds. Lavender, gold and pink. Crimson, emerald and silver. A flock of *tori*, soaring, swooping, gliding.

"See, Mrs. Naka? *We* have birds!"

Mrs. Naka's arms rose like wings. Abby caught her hands.

They flew.

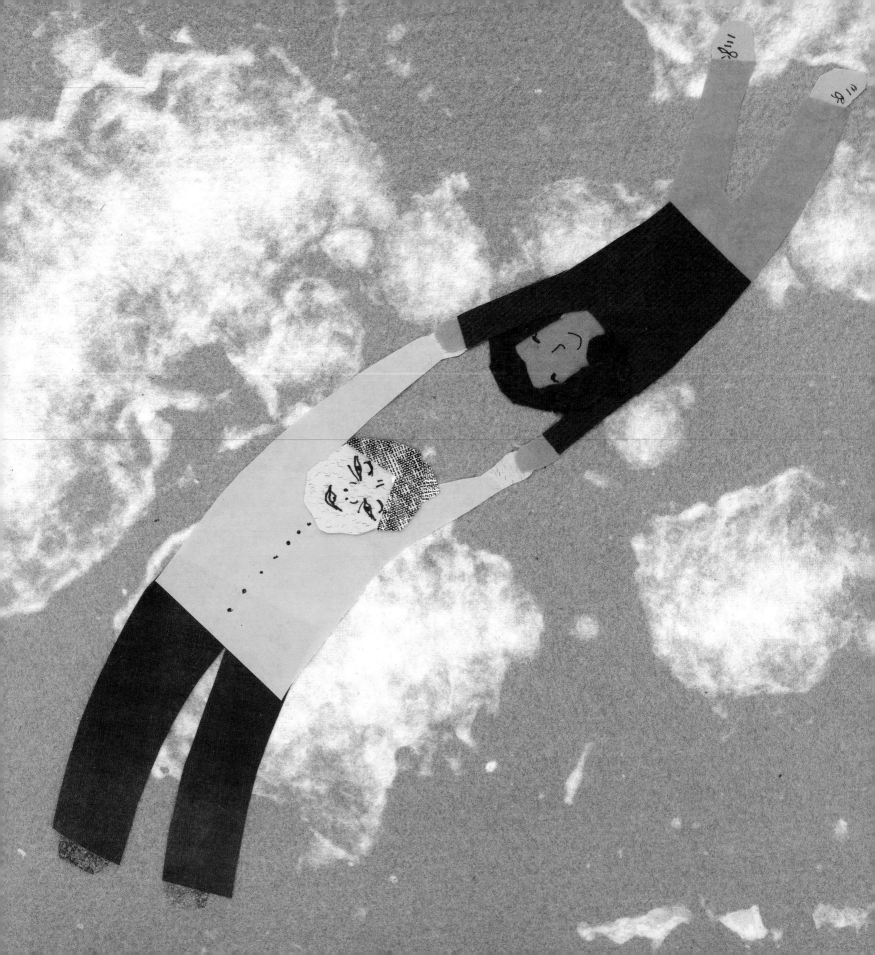